CLAUDE

on the Slopes

ALEX T. SMITH

At 112 Waggy Avenue,
there lives a dog.

A small dog.
A small, plump dog.
A small, plump dog who
wears shoes and a jumper
and a rather nifty beret.

Rather nifty beret

Jumper

Shoes

This dog is called Claude.
Hello, Claude!

He lives with Mr and Mrs Shinyshoes...

...and his best pal in the whole world, Sir Bobblysock, who is both a sock and quite bobbly.

Every day, after Mr and Mrs
Shinyshoes have hotfooted it
out of the door to work, Claude
pops on his beret and goes on
an adventure with Sir Bobblysock.

But where will they go today?

One morning (it was a Tuesday), Claude woke up in a rather loud sort of a mood.

He whistled loudly as he tied up his shoelaces. He hummed loudly as he smoothed his jumper down over his tummy.

And he said,

'Oooh! Aren't you lovely?'

loudly to himself
whilst looking in
a mirror.

So loudly in fact,
that he blew the
froth off the top
of Sir Bobblysock's frothy coffee
from the other side of the kitchen.

The reason Claude was feeling
so noisy today was because he
and Sir Bobblysock had spent
the day before (which had been
a Monday) at the library.

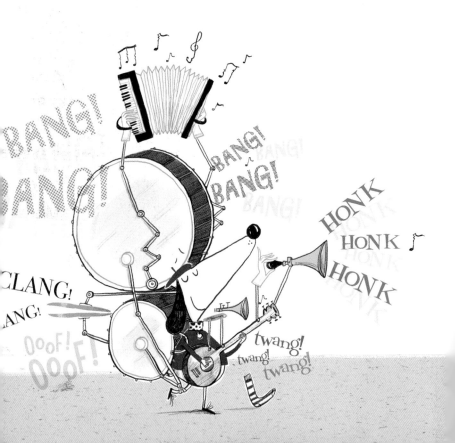

Miss Hush, the librarian, had
explained that although it was OK
to make a bit of noise in the library –
especially when you've found a very
exciting book –
turning up in your
one-man-band
outfit was a
bit much.

Jane's Hair

15 shades
of beige
Your guide to paint

Peter Pan's
People

·LIBRARY·

Then she had lost count of the number of times she'd had to remind Claude to use his nice Indoor Voice.

By the end of the day, Sir
Bobblysock had needed a
long lie down with a moist flannel.

But that was yesterday, and now
Claude needed a jolly new
adventure to go on.

'I think I'll go and get some fresh
air!' shouted Claude.

And he did.

15

Sir Bobblysock was hardly out of his bed jacket when Claude flung open the front door.

'Brrr!' Claude said, shivering. 'It's ever so chil...'

But he didn't have the chance to finish his sentence because –

Claude had slipped on a patch of
ice and flown right across the street,
landing with a bump on his bottom.

Sir Bobblysock gingerly picked
his way over to see if Claude
was all right.

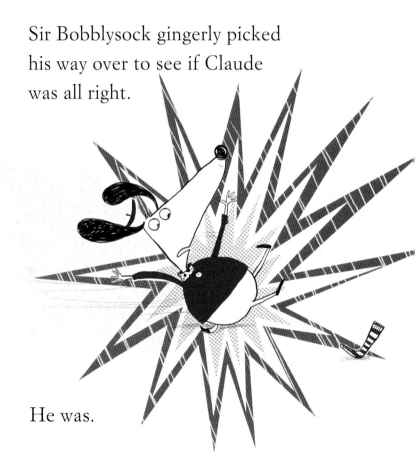

He was.

'What IS all this slippery, wet, chilly stuff?' said Claude, looking at the blanket of white that covered the street.

Then he realised – it was snow.

Claude had never seen snow for himself before, but had seen pictures in books. He was just wondering what to do with it all when suddenly someone whoooooooshed past him at a terrific speed. Then another person did. Then another.

Claude didn't know what they were doing, but he knew it was something exciting because his bottom had started to wag his tail like crazy and his eyebrows were jiggling about uncontrollably.

So he ran after them as fast
as he could.

Claude and Sir Bobblysock followed the whooshing people all the way to the Snowy Mountains' Winter Sports Centre. When they arrived, Claude and Sir Bobblysock looked about with wonder.

There was so much to see!

A cosy log cabin café,

snowy mountains,

people whizzing through the air,

and people falling over.

Claude had never played in the
snow before, so he wasn't sure what
to do. He decided to just
try and join in with what
other people were doing.
But before he and Sir
Bobblysock could do
that, they needed to
look the part.

Claude rummaged around in his beret. At last, tucked away behind the glitzy leotard Sir Bobblysock liked to wear for his keep-fit class, Claude found just the thing.

At first, Sir Bobblysock wasn't
quite sure about the earmuffs,
but once he'd looked at himself
from every angle in Claude's
handy mirror, he realised that
they brought out the colour
of his eyes beautifully.

At last Claude and Sir Bobblysock
were ready to join in the fun.

The first thing they did was join in with some children who were having a snowball fight.

Claude discovered that in a snowball fight what you do is roll up some snow into a ball and throw it at other people. What you don't do is get overexcited and throw anything you find...

That goes against the spirit of
things, especially as some people
don't really enjoy getting bopped
on the head with a flying welly...

Claude said, 'Sorry,' and gave the boy a lollipop he found in his beret. Claude thought it would be best if he found something else to do and, besides, Sir Bobblysock wasn't very keen on all those balls flying about.

32

Next, the two friends discovered
another group of people who were
doing something rather unusual
with what looked like a tea tray.
Claude and Sir Bobblysock watched
in amazement as the people zipped
down the hillside. Claude thought it
looked like terrific fun.

Sir Bobblysock thought
it looked very giddy-making
and was sure it would make him
feel a bit peculiar, so he found a
handy seat to sit on and watch, and
helped himself to a sponge finger.

Claude clambered to the top of the hill and asked the people what they were doing.

36

'We are sledging!' explained a little girl. 'Do you have a tea tray you could use?'

Well, of course Claude had a tea tray he could use. He always kept one in his beret – with a full tea service just in case there was a tea-based emergency. So he whipped it out and was ready to go!

Sledging, Claude found, was
wonderful! He liked zipping down
the hill and feeling the wind about
his ears. Sir Bobblysock told him
that his ears looked lovely when
they billowed out behind him.

Soon Claude got jolly good at sledging and everyone said he was a natural.

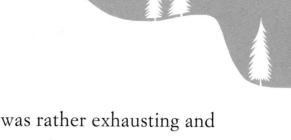

But it was rather exhausting and Claude was beginning to feel a bit mid-morning-ish and belly-rumbly, so he waved goodbye to his new friends and went to find Sir Bobblysock. But Sir Bobblysock was nowhere to be found.

Claude looked around and scratched his head. Then he noticed a rather excitable-looking crowd in the distance.

'I bet Sir Bobblysock is over there!'
Claude said to himself. He knew
that his best friend was a bit of a
nosy parker.

Claude jogged over and, sure enough, there was Sir Bobblysock in the thick of it. He'd entered himself into the Great Snowman Competition.

THE **GREAT SNOWMAN**
COMPETITION
FABULOUS PRIZES TO BE WON!

Once, when Claude and Sir
Bobblysock had been at the
beach, Sir Bobblysock had
discovered that he was a rather
talented sandcastle builder. And
snow wasn't THAT much
different from sand – that's what
Sir Bobblysock thought, anyway.

44

Claude watched, hardly daring to breathe, as Sir Bobblysock and all the other competitors started digging and rolling and sculpting the snow. But Claude needn't have worried...

ONE SOCK
AND HIS DOG

Sir Bobblysock was a dab hand and his snowman was definitely the best.

'Congratulations!' cried a rather glamorous woman in a furry outfit. 'You are the winner!' And she handed Sir Bobblysock his prizes – a silver shovel and a heated foot spa.

Claude went wild!

He whooped
and hollered in his
Outdoor Voice and
jumped up and down
on the spot.

Suddenly, out of nowhere, came a swoosh of snow. Standing behind Claude and Sir Bobblysock in a brightly coloured jacket and some snazzy goggles was a man on a pair of skis. He also had quite an extravagant moustache that Claude would have liked to have looked at more closely, but the man didn't look very happy so he thought better of it.

Instead, Claude quickly tidied up Sir Bobblysock's prizes under his beret.

'My name is Sidney Snood,' said the man, 'and I am in charge of Mountain Rescue. You were making quite a noise then, which you really mustn't do here.'

Sidney then went on to explain that whilst snow was a lot of fun, it could also be very dangerous.
If you made too much noise, all the snow at the top of the mountain could slip downwards and cover absolutely everything with more snow than was sensible.

'And that is called an avalanche,' said Sidney Snood.

Claude dragged his foot around
in circles and said, 'Sorry,' to
Sidney Snood.

Then Claude told him how nice he
thought his moustache was.

This seemed to stop Sidney Snood being cross and he smiled a big smile.

'Would you and your friend like to come and learn more about Mountain Rescue? Today I am doing a demonstration,' he said.

Claude nodded his head and wagged his tail, but Sir Bobblysock wasn't so sure. He had rather been hoping for a nice sit down and a cup of something warm, but he hopped along behind Claude because he always liked to be with his very best friend.

'We are going to pretend that this man has had an accident,' said Sidney Snood, pointing at two legs sticking out of the snow. 'I'll show you what to do.'

55

Claude and Sir Bobblysock watched as Sidney Snood calmly took a shovel out from his bag and dug and dug and dug until out clambered a rather chilly looking man.

Then Sidney Snood wrapped the
man up in a special silver, wrinkly
blanket and poured him a hot drink
from a flask.

Claude had a cup of tea too as it
had been very hard work
supervising the rescue.

Sidney turned to Claude and Sir
Bobblysock. 'So you see,' he said,
'you must be careful, because this is
the kind of accident you can cause
if you use your Outdoor Voice near
snowy mountains.'

'Now,' continued Sidney Snood in a friendly fashion, 'would you like me to teach you both how to ski?'

Claude was very excited and said,
'Yes please!' But Sir Bobblysock was
worried about his bunion, so he said
he would go and find a nice cup of
tea and watch Claude from the log
cabin at the bottom of the mountains.

Skiing, Claude
discovered, was not
as easy as riding about
on a tea tray.

It was rather tricky indeed.

Sidney showed Claude how to push himself off using the two sticks and how to bring his arms in close to his body so that he would move quicker.

He also showed him how to skid to a nice, calm stop. Claude found that in emergencies, using the nearest tree worked just as well.

After a few fall-y down sort of tries, Claude eventually got the hang of it. He skied down a small mountain and then he skied down a medium-sized mountain.

Claude found that everyone liked
to stop and watch him.

68

'As a special treat for you being so quiet all afternoon, shall we try skiing from the top of the tallest mountain?' said Sidney Snood.

Claude felt a bit giddy at the thought but said, 'OK,' and wagged his tail excitedly.

They got up the steep slope by going on a special ski lift which was really like a bench that dangled from a wire. Claude thought that it was a very fun way to travel and it didn't really matter too much if you got your skis in a tangle here and there. You could still admire the view.

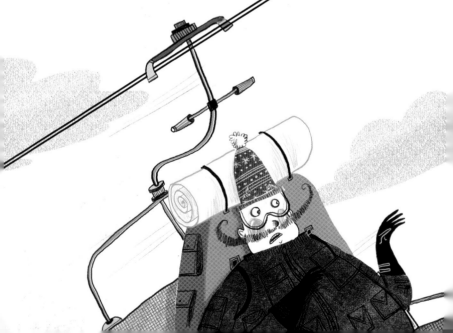

SNOWY MOUNTAIN
RULES:
No Running
and
No One-Man-Band Outfits
NO OUTDOOR VOICES

72

When they reached the top,
Claude looked down.

It was **very** high!

Claude squinted through his
binoculars. He could see Sir
Bobblysock sitting outside the log
cabin having a hot chocolate.
He was chatting to a nice young
man and showing him his bunion.

All of sudden, Claude felt ever so
giddy. It was probably from being
up so high. He suddenly desperately
wanted Sir Bobblysock to see him
all the way up at the top of the
tallest mountain so he started to
jump up and down and wave.

Then you'll never guess what he did.

He forgot all about using his Indoor Voice and shouted at the very top of his Outdoor Voice:

HELLOOOOOo
SIR BOBB

76

OOOOOOOOOOOOOOOOOOOOOO

OOOOOOOOOOOOOOOOOOOOO

SOCK!!!!

YSOCK!!!!

His voice echoed around the
mountains.

Then there was a rumble... and a
grumble...

'Uh-oh,' said Claude,
suddenly feeling a bit
bothersome about the collar.

77

A HUGE sheet of snow slipped
down from the pointiest peak and
rolled down the slope in a giant ball.

'Avalanche!'

cried Sidney Snood, as he got
wrapped up in the giant snowball
like a hotdog in a bun.

The other skiers leapt out of the way,
but down at the bottom of the
mountain, Sir Bobblysock was too
busy reading a magazine to notice
the avalanche coming his way and...

splat!

The giant avalanche snowball
splattered all over the log cabin.
Sir Bobblysock and Sidney Snood
were covered right up to their
pompoms in cold, wet snow.

'Help!' they mumbled.

There was a big problem.

Sidney Snood was the only Mountain Rescue person, and because he was right at that very moment completely covered in snow, nobody knew how to rescue him and Sir Bobblysock.

Nobody, of course, except Claude.

But how was he going to get down the tallest mountain in these silly skis, he wondered?

Then he had an idea.

Off went Claude's skis. Over his shoulder went his ski boots and then he took out his tea tray from his beret and – WHOOOOOOSH! – off went Claude down the mountain.

WHOOOOOOSH!

He was at the snow-covered cabin in seconds. Now all he needed to do was dig Sir Bobblysock and Sidney Snood out, but how? His paws were too dainty to do much digging...

Claude snapped his fingers.
He remembered Sir Bobblysock's
silver shovel prize. He had a
quick root around in his beret
until he found it and then he
dug and he dug and he dug.

Snow flew everywhere and poor Claude's arms ached. Eventually he managed to dig down to Sir Bobblysock and Sidney Snood and helped them clamber up out of the snow.

The crowd who had gathered
around to watch clapped.
'Three quiet cheers for Claude!'
whispered someone.

And everybody whispered in
their quietest Indoor Voices,

'Hooray!'

'Hooray!'

'Hooray!'

Claude went quite pink. Then
he poured Sidney a nice hot cup
of tea from his emergency tea
set and popped
Sir Bobblysock
in the heated
foot spa.

When Sidney Snood had stopped shivering he clapped Claude on the back.

'What a brave and clever dog you are!' he said. 'Won't you come and live on the Snowy Mountains and help me rescue people?'

Claude thought about it for a moment. Whizzing down the slopes was terrific fun, but he liked living in his nice warm house on Waggy Avenue too.

He looked down at Sir Bobblysock.
All the colour had gone from his
face. Claude thought they had
better go home so Sir Bobblysock
could put on his bed jacket and
recover properly with his hot water
bottle and a box of Violet Creams.
He explained all of that to Sidney,
who said that he understood.

By this time it was getting late and Claude needed to get back before Mr and Mrs Shineyshoes came home from work.

So he popped the foot spa under
his beret and said goodbye to
Sidney Snood. Then Claude and
Sir Bobblysock hopped onto their
tea tray and skeddadled home
through the snow.

Later that evening, Mr and Mrs
Shinyshoes had a surprise when
they came home from work.

'Goodness!' said Mr Shinyshoes,
'I wonder where all this snow has
come from?'

'And I wonder why Claude is fast
asleep with his feet in a foot spa?'
said Mrs Shinyshoes.

'Well, I'm sure I don't know...'
said Mr Shinyshoes.

But we do, don't we?

Fun and useful things
for snowy weather:

A snowsuit

Earmuffs

Welly boots

A tea tray for sledging

A foot spa to warm you up

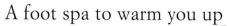